Help Came from a Stranger

by

Brenda Hyslip

DORRANCE PUBLISHING CO., INC.
PITTSBURGH, PENNSYLVANIA 15222

All Rights Reserved
Copyright © 2009 by Brenda Hyslip
No part of this book may be reproduced or transmitted
in any form or by any means, electronic or mechanical,
including photocopying, recording, or by any information
storage and retrieval system without permission in
writing from the publisher.

ISBN: 978-1-4349-0136-1
Printed in the United States of America

First Printing

For more information or to order additional books, please contact:
Dorrance Publishing Co., Inc.
701 Smithfield Street
Pittsburgh, Pennsylvania 15222
U.S.A.
1-800-788-7654
www.dorrancebookstore.com

Dedication

This saga is dedicated to the many families whose faith helped them to survive the horrors of war and to the many strangers who would risk their own lives to help others.

2010!

To Mary!

With Love

Brenda Hyphip

During World War II, a young woman and her six-year-old daughter are forced to leave Poland. Sofie is Austrian but her husband is Polish, and her child, Emma, is called a half-breed. Their journey into East Germany and finally to West Germany stretches over six years, six years of incredible hardship but also moments of pure joy as they struggle with hope, fear, faith, love, and selfishness.

Part I

Poland 1945; World War II

"Miss Sofie, you must get out of Poland. Word has it that there are only two more trains that will get people out. After that nobody knows what will happen. Please, I beg of you, take Emma and get out. You are not safe here anymore."

"Alfred, you have been a loyal friend to me and my family but my mother is in the hospital with a broken hip. I simply don't see how I can leave. Also, I am waiting for some news about my husband. The Gestapo took him ten days ago for an interrogation and I have not seen or heard from him. However, I am going back to the hospital this afternoon where I will try to talk to one of the doctors to see if my mother can travel soon. I just simply cannot leave her."

Ten days earlier…
Sofie heard loud noises and heavy knocking on the door. "Open up or we will break the door down."

"Coming, coming," the Polish maid Genja replied as she opened the door, only to find herself brutally pushed aside.

Miss Sofie, roused from all the noise and heavy knocking on the door, came out of the living room looking at the six soldiers. "What the devil is going on?" she said, looking at Genja, "and why did you let these soldiers come into this house?"

The soldier in command grabbed Sofie by the arm and pushed her back into the living room. "Be quiet," he told her. "First we need some food. We are hungry. You do have food, don't you?"

Genja looked at Sofie but Sofie nodded to the girl to go to the cellar. "Genja, there is some meat." Turning back to the man in charge, she heard herself saying, "We will have a meal for you in just a little while."

"Schnapps, we need schnapps."

"Sofie," another soldier was yelling. Sofie looked at him in disgust. "I will get you Schnapps," she told him. Then she rushed to get the glasses.

Fear, I cannot show them fear, she told herself. Even so, her fear was getting stronger by the minute. She saw the roving eyes of the men going over her body. *Please God, let them eat and leave,* she silently prayed.

Genja appeared at the door. Food was on the table.

After the meal the soldiers were getting drunk. By now one was trying to put his hand under Genja's skirt. She turned and slapped his hand but he hit her back with such force that she flew clear across the room. The soldier in charge was not taking his eyes off Sofie.

"What is going on in here?" Another voice was coming from the stairs.

"It's my mother," Sofie said. "She is an old woman. She means no harm. Just ignore her."

"Answer me. Sofie," Mother said again, looking in disgust at the soldiers, "and tell me what these men are doing in our house."

"Please, mama, go back to bed. We will be all right."

"Not until these men leave," the old woman replied.

One of the men, really drunk by now, turned to her and said, "Do you want me to help you back to bed?" poking his finger into her chest. Reacting to his insult, the old woman spat in his face, her eyes blazing.

Stunned for just a second, the soldier picked her up and threw her to the floor, kicking her with his boot in her back.

Paralyzed with fear, Sofie tried to run over to her, only to stop when she heard Genja's screams coming from the other room. Then she watched in horror as one by one the soldiers took their turn on her. "Oh, this is beginning to get boring," the soldier in charge said, looking intensely at Sofie. "We'll be back for you another time."

"Your mother has a broken hip," the doctor told Sofie later. "She will have to stay in the hospital for several weeks, I'm afraid. On older people the bones just do not heal as fast as we would like."

That was ten days ago…

"Genja, I need to go to the hospital to check on my mother. I will take Emma with me. We will be back for supper." Genja nodded her head. She had not spoken a word since the night the soldiers were at the house.

Walking along the cobblestone streets, Sofie let her mind wander. *Michael, where are you? What has happened to us? If only I knew that you are all right. I have been warned that it is too dangerous to stay here in Poland but how can I leave when I don't know where you are and with Mom in the hospital? Oh what to do. Hospital, where is the hospital? Am I crazy?* Turning around and around, she saw nothing but an old man poking his cane into the stones. "Hey Mister, where is the hospital and what happened to all the people?" But he just looked at her and shrugged.

The Red Cross, Sofie tells herself. *I am going to find out from the Red Cross. Surely they will know something.*

"Mama, I am tired." *Emma is starting to complain and I am hungry too. I want to go home now.*

"Yes, my darling, we are going home," Sofie reassured her. Then the two made their way back to their house.

At the Red Cross Station the next day, "I am so sorry, Miss Sofie," the lady from the Red Cross said. "There are no survivors. The hospital was bombed and there is nothing left. But please take Emma and get out of Poland. There is only one more train that will take people out."

"But my husband?"

"Your husband will find you later. Right now you and your daughter need to leave and get on the train to Germany. Promise me you will leave tomorrow, and may God be with you."

The next morning, "Genja, you can stay here in the house as long as you like," Sofie told the maid. "I so wish you could come with us but they are not letting Polish people on the trains anymore. Oh, this horrible war!

"Perhaps when it ends we will see each other again." They hugged each other one last time, with tears running down their faces. Then Genja turned around and went back into the house, and Sofie and Emma walked towards the train station.

There were people everywhere, yelling, crying. Sofie held Emma's hand tight. She knew if she let go for only one second they would have a hard time finding each other again.

"Your papers, Miss," a guard was asking. "Is this child yours?"

"Yes, this is Emma, my daughter," Sofie told him.

"All right then." He pointed to the train that was going to East Germany.

"Thank you sir." Holding Emma's hand even tighter, mother and daughter climbed up the stairs and onto the train.

How many times in the last two days have we been ordered to get off the train for paper check? Sofie had lost count. Emma finally went to sleep in Sofie's arms. *Maybe it won't be too much longer and we will be over the border into East Germany,* were her last thoughts and then she also drifted off into sleep.

Loud voices…everybody off the train.

Paper check…the soldier who was checking Sofie and Emma's papers whistled to another soldier to come over. They both studied the papers, then one of them tried to take Emma from Sofie. "She is going onto another train," he told her.

"No, this is my child. We will not be separated." She was holding onto Emma for dear life, and screaming from the top of her lungs.

"What is going on here?" Another soldier with more stripes on his uniform walked toward them. He looked at Sofie and Emma's papers closely. *Mother Austrian, father Polish, child born in Poland, hmm.* He looked from Sofie to Emma, then turned to the others, who were waiting for his decision, and said to let the girl stay with her mother, she is a half-breed.

Little did Sofie know that Emma's life was spared in this minute or that the train was going to Auschwitz to the concentration camp. Little did she know.

Two more days on trains and finally they came to a stop. Everybody was told to get off. "We are spending the night here and tomorrow we will continue the journey," one of the soldiers told them.

"Look. Emma, we are getting something to eat." The soup tasted like salty water, but oh, it was hot and they were even given a piece of bread. Half an hour later they were ushered into what looked like a huge barn with straw on the floor. *Oh, we can finally stretch out,* Sofie thought. Then she put her arms around Emma and both fell into a deep sleep. Some time later…

"What is that noise, what is happening here?" Emma was waking up.

Sofie put her hand over Emma's mouth. "*Shh* darling, please don't make a sound, we have to be very, very still." She watched as a soldier shone a flashlight into people's faces, but he passed them by. Then he saw something he liked; it was a young woman. And Sofie watched in horror as he dragged her by the arm out of the building.

"Oh dear God," Sofie murmured, "Oh dear God," afraid to breathe or go back to sleep. Morning finally came and everybody was ordered back onto the train.

Two more long days and nights and Sofie, Emma, and about sixty other people were ordered off the train. They looked around and saw what seemed to be a fairly small town on the east side of Germany. They were sent into a large building where again they had to stand in line for paper check. On one side were the town people, mostly farmers, and one by one families got assigned to them.

When Sofie was called, a woman in her early thirties took one look at Sofie and Emma, shook her head to the officer, and said, "What am I to do with them? I need field hands. I have no use for them."

The officer shook his head and told her, "You will take them, give them room and board, and put them to work. Move over and go with her," he barked at Sofie. Then he yelled, "Next."

Sofie held Emma's hand tight and slowly walked behind the woman through the streets and up to the farm. Finally there, they were shown a tiny room with a bed, a table, two chairs, and a small stove. There was a tiny window, even dirtier than the room. "Here we are," the woman said to Sofie. "Settle in and when you are done come downstairs, meet the field hands, and get something to eat."

Sofie sat down on the bed, tears streaming down her face in total despair, until six-year-old Emma pulled on her hand and said, "Come, mama, I am hungry." Sofie had no choice and both mother and daughter walked down the creaky wooden stairs to find the kitchen.

Sitting around a long table were two women and four men. Sofie introduced herself and Emma. The older of the women told Sofie to sit down and said, "I am Ana. I cook the food for us and the animals. This is Lela, she cleans the stalls. This is Franz, he takes care of the horses. The three of us live on the farm. The other three men come every morning to work in the fields. Now eat before the stew gets cold."

Emma dug right in but Sofie was so tired she barely touched the food. Afterwards, Ana told Sofie, "Miss Wally wants to talk to you before you go back to your room." Looking at Sofie with kind eyes, she added, "My room is across from yours and if you need anything, don't be afraid to knock on my door." Sofie thanked her and then walked with Emma toward the main house.

"Isn't this beautiful," Emma cried as she stepped inside. "Look, mama, this is like our house back home." They found Wally sitting in a beautiful soft chair near the fire with a silver tray of cakes on the table next to her. Emma stared at the pastry, but said nothing.

Wally watched the child, but also said nothing. Then she turned to Sofie and said, "There is some wood in your stove. You need to make a fire. The nights get bitter cold here and tomorrow you can go to the back and cut some wood for yourself. Also see Ana in the morning so you can help her with the chores."

The next morning...

"Mama, I am freezing," Emma whined. The small fire had gone out overnight.

"I know, darling it's cold. we will go down and get something to eat and then will see about getting some wood." After breakfast, which consisted of bread and a spread made of lard, Sofie headed toward the back of the farm to see about the wood but all she could see were very large tree trunks.

"You'll have to split it yourself," said one of the field hands as he walked by on his way to his chores.

Sofie looked at the ax, tears streaming down her face again, thinking, *oh Michael, where are you? Emma and I need you so,* but there was no answer. Sofie tried to work with the ax, but there was no hope, the wood just would not split.

Emma watched her mother, then turned around and ran as fast as she could towards the main house. She did not even bother to knock but yelled, "Miss Wally, Miss Wally, come quick, mama is in trouble."

Wally got up from her table. "What's wrong?" but Emma grabbed her by the hand and pulled her out the door toward the woodpile. Halfway there Wally saw what she thought was the most pitiful sight she had ever seen in her life. There stood this tiny woman with this big ax in her hand, tears streaming down her face.

She has never done anything like this in her life, she thought to herself. *What in God's name am I going to do with her?* Then her gaze fell onto Emma, whose little hand was still holding on to her, and something very soft welled up in her. "Come with me into the house," she told Sofie, trying to hide her emotions, and with that the three of them walked back to the main house.

There the two women sat down and talked and Wally learned a little bit of what had happened to them. "My husband has also been fighting the war for the last four years," she told Sofie, "and I have not had word from him in over two years. But enough of this for now. Let's see what you can do."

And so it was that Sofie took care of Wally's house, helped Ana with the lighter chores, and pitched in wherever she was needed. Wally often told her, "I just cannot imagine how I ever got along without you," and because of that the two women slowly became friends.

Months went by. Sofie waited desperately to hear some news about Michael and Wally was also waiting to hear anything about her husband and her brother who was now reported missing in action.

Finally Sofie received a letter from the Red Cross addressed to her. With shaking fingers she tried to open it. "What, mama, what does it say?" Emma was jumping up and down.

"The Red Cross has located your grandma, your papa's mom. She is on the West side of Germany and also has been trying to find us. Also two of my brothers are on the West side. This is such wonderful news; let's go and share it with Wally." Both women ran down the stairs to the living room. "Oh my God, what has happened?" Wally looked like a white statue, tears running down her face, holding a telegram in her hands.

"Wally, why are you crying?" Emma asked her but Wally could not speak. She just handed the paper to Sofie. *Died a hero for the fatherland* was all it said. It was the coldest letter Sofie had ever seen.

She gently put her arms around Wally and said, "I will make us some tea." When she came back with the tea she found Emma kneeling in front of Wally with her head in her lap as Wally gently stroked her hair.

Sofie sat down and put her letter with the good news deep into her shirt pocket. Not a word was spoken for a very long time.

After that day, Wally spent every free minute she had with Emma. The two became inseparable. Sofie often felt a little left out but then felt guilty for her jealousy. Emma had lost so much and they were really lucky that they were treated with so much kindness.

Another few months went by. Wally seemed to be doing better, when one day she cried, "Sofie! I have gotten news from my brother. He had been a prisoner of war but they have set him free; he will be here tomorrow. We must have a special dinner for him, but I am leaving all of it up to you. I am too excited to help with anything. Come, Emma, help me pick out my best dress, this is such a happy day!"

"Everything looks so beautiful, Sofie. I could have never done this," Wally said later. "But what, only two plates? You and Emma must join us. I am much too happy to take no for an answer."

"Oh Marcus, welcome home!" Wally was hugging this tall handsome man, then went on, saying, "This is Sofie and Emma. They are as close to me as family." Marcus looked at Sofie, this beautiful tiny woman, and something stirred inside of him so powerful that it almost took his breath away. Never in his life had he felt like this about any other woman. Wally watched her brother closely. "Let's go and eat," she said cheerfully. "This is truly a beautiful day."

"Your practice is waiting for you," Wally told Marcus later. "The old doctor is doing his best but the town needs you desperately." And so it was.

Every free minute Marcus could spare he spent at Wally's so he could be near Sofie. "You know he is in love with you," she told Sofie one day, "and he would be a good father to Emma."

"I know," Sofie replied, "but Wally, I am not free and there is no news about Michael. I simply cannot give up hope that he is alive. Oh, damn this war, damn this war!"

Lice

Months went by. Emma was now seven years old and loved school. Sofie usually tried to walk at least half of the way to pick her up. Emma always had stories to tell about her day. Today, she had just left the farm when she saw Emma running toward her. Her face was glowing with excitement. "Mama, Mama, I have the most wonderful news."

"What, Emma, what?" Sofie looked at the child.

"I have lice, I have lice." Emma was dancing around her. "The whole school is closed for three days. No school! Everybody has lice."

Oh dear God, Sofie thought. "Emma, what happened?"

"Mama, that one family over by the river has them and they gave them to all of us. I am just so happy." Sofie just looked at Emma in panic, but she did not say anything. Her mind was racing. Emma had very long blond hair braided into two beautiful braids. *What am I going to do,* she thought. *I don't have anything to get rid of them. Marcus, I need to see Marcus,* she told herself. *He will know what to do.*

On their way to the doctor's office they saw Marcus walking toward them, carrying his medical bag. Before Sofie could speak he told her, "I know, I have already heard about the lice and I have already made a paste to put on her hair. She is going to hate it but it will kill the lice."

Sofie took his hand. "Marcus, thank you. Sometimes I just don't know what we would do without you."

"You could marry me," he replied softly. She did not know how to answer so they walked quietly back to the farm.

"We need to bring the wooden bathtub into the house, we need lots of hot water and towels." Wally was going around giving orders and everybody was running around helping until they finally had Emma sitting in the tub.

Sofie washed her hair and then they put the paste on her head. It smelled like tar. Emma cried, "Stop, stop, I am getting sick!"

"No you won't," Sofie told her. She felt sick herself, but she had to put on a brave face in front of Emma. "We'll wrap some towels around it, the paste has to stay on an hour."

It was the longest hour, but finally it was over. "We will wash it out now, Emma," she coaxed the child. "See, it wasn't so bad."

"Yes it was," Emma said. "Yes it was. I don't think having lice is as much fun as I thought it was." Sofie did not have the heart to tell her that they had to do it two more times.

We'll face that tomorrow, she told herself. In the meantime Wally told Ana to go and get all the sheets and blankets out of their room. They also had to be washed with the rest of their towels and clothing. "You will have to sleep with me in the main house," Wally told Sofie. "We cannot dry everything quickly enough."

"Thank you, Wally." Sofie looked at her gratefully and then she thanked God for this woman.

Two more days, two more times. It was an ordeal for all of them, but that also came to pass. Emma's hair was healthy again and soon things went back to normal.

Siberian Winter

"We are going to have a very cold winter this year." Sofie, Wally, Marcus, and Emma were sitting in Wally's living room, the only room in the house that was warm. "We don't have much coal left. Everything is rationed so much and nobody is allowed to cut any trees down. I am really worried. Maybe it won't be so bad," Marcus said. Sofie could tell that he was worried too. They were right. Mid-October turned so cold the ice on the windows was two inches thick and that was just the beginning. It started snowing and continued to snow. The well was frozen solid. No water; everybody gathered ice and snow in buckets and took it into the house to melt, because the animals had to have some water to survive. This went on for weeks.

Often Sofie and Emma spent eight hours a day in bed, but even though they were wearing every stitch of clothing they owned they still could not get warm. Emma never stopped shivering, so one mid-morning Sofie got them both out of bed. "Come on, Emma," she said to the child. "We are going into the woods and see if we cannot find something to make a fire." With a blanket under her arm they went to the back of the barn where Sofie had seen an old sled. She then found a small saw and mother and child made their way toward the woods. There was nothing, nothing. The ground looked like a white carpet.

"Mama there is no wood," Emma whined.

"Well then," Sofie said, "we will cut down a tree." She took the saw and started to work on the smallest little tree she could see. It was almost impossible. The trunk was frozen, but Sofie would not give up. They were going to have a fire. Finally that was done and in pieces that would fit onto their small sled. Then she covered the wood with the blanket and they made their way back to the farm.

They passed only one old man. Everybody who did not have to be out stayed in their homes. Sofie panicked for a second but the old man just stared for a second at the sled, then he nodded to Sofie and went on his way. *He knows,* Sofie thought, *he knows what is on that sled,* but she was so happy to have the wood she really did not care.

"Oh dear God." Wally was standing outside her door with the most panicked look on her face. "Do you have any idea what will happen to you if you get caught cutting wood?"

"But Wally, I did not get caught. We are going to have a fire today. Let's just be warm for one night." And so they sat around the stove. It felt wonderful. They also heated three bricks, wrapped them, and put them into their beds, and when everybody finally went to their rooms, Sofie thanked God a thousand times for this day.

The next morning: "Mama, get up." Emma tried to shake her. "Why won't you get up?"

Sofie tried to open her eyes but she did not seem to be able to. "I cannot open my eyes, Emma. Go, run and get Wally."

"Your eyes are open, Mama," Emma said, looking at her in confusion, but without another word she left the room to find Wally.

Wally could not believe what she was seeing. "I cannot open my eyes," Sofie told her. "I don't even feel them. What is happening?"

"Mama, your eyes are wide open," Emma told Sofie again, but Wally put her finger on Emma's lips to quiet the child.

Then she told Sofie, "You just lie still. I am going to get Marcus. He will fix you some medicine. I'll be back as soon as I can."

Emma stay with Mama. "I need to talk to Wally," Marcus told the child. "We'll be back soon and I will have a surprise for you for being such a good helper.

"I am afraid she will be blind—her corneas appear to be frozen," Marcus told Wally a little while later, "but it is really too soon to tell. I will do everything in my power, but you need to be prepared for the worst."

Five weeks later, Sofie still could not see anything. Emma got restless; she was tired of being cooped up. So one day her little temper flared and she yelled at Sofie. "If you had not gone out to cut the stupid wood, you would not have frozen your eyes! This is all your fault. I heard Marcus tell Wally that you will never see again."

Sofie listened to her daughter and then she felt something running down her cheeks. *A tear—where did it come from? If there is a tear, there is life,* were her last thoughts before she went into a coma.

One week later, Wally, Emma, and Ana had spent every free minute by Sofie's bedside, but there was no change. Marcus also came over every morning and evening, but he also had given up hope. They were just about to leave Sofie's room when Emma yelled, "Look, Mama is waking up. I saw her move her hands."

And sure enough, Sofie started to move and slowly tried to open her eyes. "Where am I?" she said, looking confused.

"You're in your bed," Marcus told her. "You just took a little nap."

Sofie started to remember. "I can see you, it's a little foggy, but I can see you."

"We have just witnessed a miracle," Marcus said to Wally, who stood like a statue, not believing what they had just witnessed. Every day Sofie's vision got clearer and about two weeks later, life went on as if nothing had ever happened.

The Dolls

February. The days were getting a little bit warmer and most of the time they could get water from the well. Emma's birthday was at the end of February. She was going to be ten and Wally and Sofie were trying to figure out what to do to make it a special day. "I know," Wally said one day. I just had the greatest idea. Let's go up into the attic. There are trunks up there. Maybe we can find something in them that we can give to Emma. "And so they did."

"I've got it, Sofie come over here. I found the perfect gift." Sofie heard Wally yelling and then she saw it. It was a doll, a very large doll. A rag doll, except for the head that was made out of some kind of plaster. "It's a boy," Wally said, bursting with pride. "He just needs to be cleaned up and clothed."

Sofie studied the doll, but then Wally's excitement spread over to her. "You are right, Wally, we will clean him up and I will try to make him a pair of pants and a shirt."

Every evening after Emma had gone to sleep, the two women sat together and worked on the doll. Even Ana got caught up in the excitement. One evening she came into the room holding a pair of boots she had knitted for the doll. "My contribution," she said proudly.

Finally they were done. "Not bad, ladies, not bad," Marcus told them. "I cannot wait to see Emma's face when she sees her present."

"Emma, you must go to sleep now. Tomorrow is your birthday and you don't want to be tired." Sofie needed to go back down to the kitchen where Wally and Ana waited for her. They wanted to get to work and decorate Emma's birthday cake.

Finally that was done too. The cake was on the table and the doll sat proudly in the chair when Sofie came down with Emma the next morning. Everybody was in the room, even the field hands, singing "Happy Birthday." Emma's eyes were shining like two blue stars and then she saw the doll and said, "Mama, I have a doll! I really have a doll!" She ran over to the chair to touch it.

"It's a boy," Wally said, "and he is waiting for you to give him a name." It took Emma a few seconds. Then she said in a firm voice, "Hansel, his name will be Hansel." She did not care about eating cake or looking at any of the other small gifts, she only had eyes for Hansel.

"I think we did good," Wally said, looking from Sofie to Ana. "Yes, I think we did good."

Emma and Hansel were inseparable through the summer except for school, where she could not take him. The doll simply did not leave her sight. Sofie often watched her daughter, thinking, *oh, how I wish your daddy was here with us so maybe you could have had a brother or sister,* but there was still no news of any kind about Michael.

Fall was here again and Christmas was fast approaching. Wally had a little more flour and sugar this year. The crop had been better than in previous years. They were even allowed to butcher a pig. "We are going to have the best Christmas ever," she announced one day. "We will have meat, we will have baked cookies, and we will have a Christmas tree." Everybody got caught up in the excitement; it was a magical month. Finally Christmas Eve came.

"I cannot eat a bite," Emma said.

"You have to eat," Sofie told her. "First we eat, then we read a few verses from the Bible. We will sing some Christmas songs and then we will wait for the bell to ring and the door to the Christmas Room to open." Nobody had seen the tree except Wally and Sofie. That room had been locked for the last two weeks. During the last song, Sofie and Wally had quietly disappeared.

Finally the lights were turned off, the bell rang, and the door to the Christmas Room opened. Nobody made a sound. It was pure magic. All they could see was the most beautiful Christmas tree they thought they had ever seen. The wax candles were burning bright and the simple homemade decorations looked like bright stars that had fallen from the sky. Then they opened presents. They were simple things. Hansel had a new outfit, Ana got some new gloves, Wally some new socks, and Marcus was showing off his new scarf that Sofie had knitted for him.

Then Emma just stared at the new doll that was sitting under the tree. It was a girl doll. Her porcelain face was exquisite. "Oh, mama," Emma said. "She has real hair and eyelashes. Isn't she the most beautiful doll?"

"Yes, she is," Sofie said happily. Then she squeezed Marcus's hand because he was the one who had found her.

"Karin," Emma said, her eyes shining.

"Her name is Karin."

"You have another baby," Sofie reminded Emma, pointing to Hansel, but Emma paid no attention to him. She only had eyes for the new doll. Later, Sofie reminded Emma again, "You have two babies. You need to show some love to Hansel too," but Emma again ignored her mother. She only wanted Karin.

Finally the evening ended and everybody went to their room to get some sleep. Emma made a bed for the new doll and went to sleep.

Christmas morning…
Where was Hansel? He was gone. Only Karin was in her little bed. "Mama, where is Hansel?" Emma finally asked.

"He has gone away," Sofie told the child. "You did not love him last night. I don't think he wants to live here anymore."

"I don't care," Emma told her. "I have Karin now. I don't need Hansel." By early afternoon Sofie noticed the change in Emma. She was very quiet; some of the joy from the night before had gone out of her. Sofie did not ask what was wrong. Deep down she knew the problem, but Emma had to work this one out by herself.

During the night…
What was that sound? Emma was crying uncontrollably. "Why are you crying, Emma," Sofie asked her daughter.

"I want my Hansel," Emma whispered. "I know I was a bad mama to him last night, but I love him as much as I love Karin. I want him to come back home."

Sofie's heart was aching to see her child suffer so, but she also knew that Emma had just learned a very harsh lesson. "Pray to God, Emma, to send Hansel back. God will hear you," and so Emma did.

The next morning Emma opened her eyes and could not believe what she was seeing. In the chair next to her bed she saw Hansel sitting next to Karin. "Oh Hansel, you came back to me," she cried and then she picked him up in one arm and Karin in the other. Her whole world was perfect again.

The Dream

Emma was almost eleven now and Sofie still had not heard any news about Michael. Every time they heard about a train coming through which could possibly carry some soldiers that had been released Sofie and all the other women gathered around the train station, hoping to see one of their loved ones.

But once again nothing. Sofie had looked in every soldier's face, but all she had seen were tired, unfamiliar eyes staring back at her.

"Maybe Michael will be on the next train." Wally was trying to cheer her up. "No news means hope," she added.

"I know, Wally," Sofie replied. "It is just so hard and it has been so long. I just wish I knew if Michael was alive."

A few nights later, Sofie woke up in the middle of the night drenched in sweat. It took her a few minutes to realize where she was and what had just happened.

It was summer, a beautiful day and Sofie was sitting by a large pond, staring into the water.

What was that? The water turned crystal clear in front of her eyes and she saw Michael's face coming toward her. "Oh Michael," Sofie cried and started to stretch out her arms to help him out of the water. Their hands touched for a few seconds but Sofie could not hold onto him slowly, their fingers separated as Sofie watched in horror Michael's face sinking deeper and deeper into the water, until there was nothing left to see. "No," Sofie cried, "no, no," and then she woke up.

"Mama, are you all right?" She heard Emma's voice. Sofie's cries had awakened her.

"Yes, Emma, go back to sleep, Mama just had a dream, everything is all right." Nothing was all right. Sofie realized Michael had died that night. He had just said good-bye to her. If she had only been able to pull him out of the water. If she had only had more strength to hold on to him.

After all, it was only a dream, but deep in her heart she knew the truth. Michael was dead, he wanted her to know, and she knew the truth. Sofie told nobody about the dream, not even Wally, and especially Marcus. She knew Marcus loved her, but she did not want to give him any hope that they could possibly have a future together. After all, there was no real proof that Michael was dead, Sofie told herself. Even so, she knew better in her heart.

The Principal

Another year went by. Emma was twelve years old now, and still loved school. Sofie, whenever she could, walked down to the school to pick her up. Today she stood waiting outside the classroom. Then the principal came out of his office and asked her to step inside. "Is Emma all right?" Sofie asked nervously.

"Yes, yes, Emma is fine," the principal told her. "I need to talk to you about another matter. It has come to our attention that in all the years that you have lived here, you have not joined the Communist Party, not even the women's organization. Let me tell you that we receive a list about every three to six months with names that have not joined or supported the Furher's party. Therefore, the Fatherland assumes that you are not a friend. Can you give me reason why that is so?"

Sofie stood in shock, but then anger welled up in her and she told the principal, "I have lost my husband because he was Polish and my only child was almost taken away from me because she was born in Poland. I will never join this party or any other party."

The principal studied her closely, but then he continued telling her. "You have no idea what consequences this could have for you. However, let me make you a proposition. You could show some gratitude every now and then to me and some of my colleagues and I would make your name disappear as long as you please us.

"You want me to prostitute myself," Sofie said. "I will never do that"—yelling now. "Not for you or your fatherland." She was shaking with rage. Then she added, "You are a swine!"

"You will live to regret this," the principal told her. His face was now deep red with anger. Then he pointed to the door and Sofie found herself excused. She found Emma.

"Mama are you all right? You look so pale," Emma asked her. Sofie nodded and squeezed Emma's hand. She could not utter a word. She felt a fear coming over her that she had not felt in a very long time.

Two months later…
"Miss Sofie, I need to speak to you in private." It was the principal's wife.

"Come in and sit down. What is it, are you all right?" Sofie asked the woman.

I know about my husband's conversation with you about joining the Communist Party. I also know how you reacted to his proposition. You are not the first that this happened to, nor will you be the last, but you are the first to have had the courage to turn him down. I don't know my husband any more, and I have stopped loving him years ago. I do not agree with anything he and his colleagues are doing, but we have five children that I cannot leave behind. But let me tell you what my husband does, and if he ever found out what I am about to do, I would be executed. Every three months my husband does get a list with names of people who will be sent to Siberia, never to return, and your name is on that latest list. Only you will be sent, Emma will stay here. You will have to leave in the next twenty-four hours or it will be too late.

"I have a brother who has connections to smuggle people from the east side of Berlin to the west side. I have already talked to him about your situation. He is willing to help. Do you have any money? This is not cheap and there are no guarantees."

Sofie stood frozen with fear as she continued to listen to the woman. "I have money saved," she heard herself saying.

"Good then," the principal's wife said. "I will let my brother know. It will have to be done quickly. Be ready to leave by tomorrow night. I will get last instructions to you on what to do some time tomorrow morning." Then she left as if nothing had happened.

Sofie walked as if she were in a coma, straight to Wally's quarters. She knew she could trust her and so she told her almost word for word about the conversation that had just happened between her and the principal's wife.

Wally's face became white. *I am losing Emma,* was her first thought. *I could report this and maybe get to keep Emma,* but instantly she scolded herself. Her brother would never forgive her, Emma would never forgive her, and most of all, God would never forgive, and she herself, would never be able to make this right. She looked at Sofie, who did not know what to do. "We'll face it tomorrow," she went on, "but first we are going to have a wonderful dinner tonight. I will call Marcus. You must leave everything to me.

"Go rest a while. You will need your strength in the following days." Sofie just looked at her, but Wally pushed her out the door. "Go rest, Emma and I will cook."

So with that, Sofie went upstairs, but she could not sleep. Instead she counted her money, made sure that all of her papers were together, got the old worn suitcase, and put only the bare necessities in it. A change of clothes for Emma, nothing for herself, because that was all the little suitcase would hold.

Evening came. Wally had outdone herself. There was a roast, new potatoes, and an assortment of vegetables and freshly baked bread. Marcus was there and had it not been for the news earlier, you would have thought that it was a festive occasion.

Nothing was mentioned during the meal, but later, after Emma had gone to sleep, the dark reality set back in.

Marcus handed Sofie an envelope and said, "Here is some money, Sofie. It will come in handy for you."

Sofie looked inside the envelope. "Marcus," she cried, "I cannot take this, it is too much."

"Shuh, shuh." He put his fingers on her lips. "I don't need much myself," he told her, "and I cannot think of a better way than to try and help you."

Sofie placed a kiss on his cheek. "Thank you, Marcus." Then they turned away from each other, both with tears in their eyes. *I could have loved him,* Sofie thought, *had I been free.* Then she closed the door and went upstairs.

Mid-morning the principal's wife came by as promised with the instructions for Sofie. She was to leave that night.

"Why do I have to take a bath and go to bed so early?" Emma complained later that evening. "Just do as I tell you, Emma," Sofie told her. "I will explain it all to you later."

Something woke Emma up. At the foot of her bed she saw a very large figure. Was she really awake or was she dreaming? She closed her eyes and opened them several times but the outline of this figure would not disappear. Emma now fully realized that she was awake. Why wasn't she afraid? A very soothing calmness came over her, and even so the figure did not speak, Emma felt as if it was saying, "Please do not be afraid. I will be with you." Years later this same figure would appear to Emma again to let her know it would be watching over her. With that, Emma went into a sound sleep.

Midnight...
"Why do I have to get up, Mama? It is still dark outside."

"Just hurry and get dressed," Sofie told her. With that, the two women left the farm that had been their home for many years. Sofie and Wally had said their tearful goodbyes the night before, but Sofie knew that Wally was watching them leave from behind the dark windows.

"I cannot walk another step," Emma whined. "I want to go home, back to bed."

"Just walk, Emma. We have to go over to the next town to catch the train."

So they walked...

After four hours, they finally reached the train station. A tall man walked toward them and told Sofie, "I am here to meet you. I know you are afraid, but you need to trust me. I have all the necessary papers. We are traveling as husband and wife and if we get stopped, let me do all the talking. We should arrive in East Berlin in about five hours."

The train ride was uneventful. There was only one paper check and it went smoothly. Sofie was sick with fear, but did not let Emma see it. Finally they arrived at their destination. "We are now going to my home," the man told Sofie. "My wife is waiting for us. You will stay with us one night and tomorrow we will try to get you to the West side, where you will be safe."

Very early the next morning, the guide told Sofie, "We have to cross the border when there are a lot of people on the train. You and Emma will be by yourself, but I will be just a few feet away. Do not look at me. If something goes wrong, I will try to intervene. If asked where you are going, say you have a sick sister in the hospital, and you need to visit her with your one-day pass." Then he added, "and whatever you do, don't look nervous. The guard will pick up on that right away and everything will be lost.

"The crossing will only take about forty-five minutes." And with those last words, they boarded the train.

"Paper check, paper check," the guard yelled as he walked through the aisles of the train. *Oh dear God,* Sofie prayed silently, but the guard just smiled at Emma and walked by.

The next thing Sofie felt was a strong hand touching her shoulder and her guide whispering to her. "You can breathe now, we are on the West side, you are safe.

"I will get off the train at the next stop to go back home. Remember what I told you to do next," were his last words, and then he was gone.

"Mama, why are you crying?"

"These are happy tears, Emma, happy tears." Hours later they did arrive at the shelter the guide told them to go to, and stood in line to be processed.

The lady behind the desk took all of Sofie's and Emma's real papers, which had been sewn into Sofie's coat lining. "You can never go back. You do know that," she said, and Sofie nodded her head. Then after she had all the necessary information, she gave them the address of a camp where they needed to stay until they had a chance to get out of Berlin. "I gave you one of the nicer camps," she added as she stroked over Emma's hair.

Berlin seemed so large and confusing, but finally they arrived at the camp which would become their new home for nine weeks. Again they stood in a long line, but finally they were assigned to their room.

"You are very lucky," Sofie was told. "We have two cots in a room available that only holds eight people. You also have a sink in that room. There is a little walk to the bathrooms, but most of the rooms hold between twenty and thirty cots and no sink. There is a mess hall downstairs. You will get three meals a day, and an infirmary on the other side of the building with a doctor on staff. We will also get in touch with your mother-in-law, and if she is willing to take you in, you could be out of Berlin in two to three months." With that, Sofie and Emma were excused.

Mother and daughter were stone tired as they made their way to their room. "Mama, I don't want to eat," Emma told her, but Sofie knew they had to. It had been about ten hours since either one of them had any kind of nourishment. The evening meal consisted of two pieces of bread, some cheese, and a cup of milk for Emma. Water for Sofie, but all of it tasted like the best meal they had ever had.

When they got back to their room, the other families sat on their cots and stared at them. Sofie introduced herself and Emma. Then they layed down on their cots and went into a heavy sleep. The next morning a woman gently shook Sofie. "You need to get up and get breakfast. Otherwise the mess hall will be closed and you will have to wait until lunch to get something to eat." Sofie thanked her and down they went. So this became their routine, day in and day out.

Weeks went by, and it was a beautiful day. Emma kept begging Sofie. "Please, mama, can't we go out a little bit, walk around and look at all the shops?"

Sofie hesitated. She had been warned not to leave the camp, but Emma's eyes pleaded with her so she gave in. She felt restless herself. "All right," she told her daughter. "We will go out for a couple of hours." She silently told herself, *what could it hurt? We just have to be very careful.*

They looked into every window. They could not buy anything—all their money had been taken away from them when they had arrived at the camp—but they did not care, they had too much fun just looking.

Russian Tanks

What was happening? People started running, screaming, and falling to the ground. Bullets were flying next to Sofie's head. Then she saw it. Russian tanks were lined up on the other side of the street, which turned out to be the East side, shooting into the West side. "Run, Emma, run!" Sofie yelled as more bullets were flying and so they ran with all the other people, where to, they had no idea. Finally Sofie found herself pushed inside one of the large ruins where people lay bleeding. *Emma, where is Emma?* Sofie looked around in panic. "Emma," she cried again.

"Mama, Mama, I am here!" She then heard this tiny little voice.

"Oh Emma, you are bleeding."

"No mama, this is blood from the girl who stood next to me." *Oh dear God thank you,* Sofie prayed, *thank you.*

After what seemed to be hours, it got very quiet outside and one by one people left the ruins. When Sofie and Emma got back to their camp, the lady who had checked them looked at their bloody clothes, but she said nothing. Sofie hung her head in shame. Why didn't she listen? Why did they venture out, why, why?

Three more weeks went by. They had now been in Berlin six weeks. Six very long weeks.

One morning Sofie was called into the office. "We have very good news for you. We heard from your mother-in-law. She is more than happy to take you in, so now we can prepare papers for you to leave Berlin." Then she added, "You are so very fortunate to have someone living on the West side. Some families have been here for over three years. Hopefully we can get you out in three to four more weeks."

The Fever

Scarlet fever: Two teenage girls in their room came down with it. It was like a raging inferno throughout the camp. Ambulances were coming and going around the clock, picking up people and taking them to the hospitals. So many dead! Nobody ever returned from the hospital. It was the worst epidemic. Sofie was afraid even to go to the bathrooms. Nobody spoke or got close to anybody else.

News came for Sofie. *Your papers are ready. You are scheduled to fly out of Berlin in four days.* Sofie could hardly breathe. *Finally we are getting out,* she smiled to herself, but it turned out to be not as simple as she thought.

Emma had no appetite. She became listless. "Mama, I want to stay in bed," she told Sofie. "I don't feel so good."

Sofie touched her head. She felt hot. Sofie panicked. *Oh dear God, please don't let her have the fever.* "We will go down to the infirmary first thing in the morning," she told Emma as she tucked her into her blankets.

The night was endless, but morning came and Sofie took Emma to see the doctor.

"She's coming down with scarlet fever," the doctor told Sofie. "We need to send her to the hospital."

"No, you can't send her to the hospital!" Sofie pleaded. "Nobody ever comes back! Our papers are ready, we are to fly out the day after tomorrow. Please, doctor, please don't send her to the hospital, she won't come back."

The doctor listened carefully. His heart went out to her. Then he pointed to an isolated table. "Let's sit down so we can talk without being heard." Sofie sat down, holding Emma close, and listened to what the doctor had to say. He told her, "I will give your child an injection to get the fever down. I want you to put her to bed, then bring her back in the morning for another, and that night for another. Talk to nobody about this. I could lose my license. If anybody suspects that she is not well, they will not let her on the plane. The minute you get to your destination, she needs to see a doctor. I will give you a letter tomorrow night when you bring her down for her last shot. Now go back to your room, put her to bed, and pray that her fever stays down."

Sofie went back to their room to put Emma to bed. Her heart was heavy, but then she prayed and prayed until she finally went to sleep.

Morning came. Emma's fever seemed to be down for now. Sofie dressed them both; then the two went down to have a little breakfast. Emma refused to eat, but Sofie coaxed her to drink a little milk. Then they went to get their final instructions for their departure.

Now, one more time to see the doctor. Emma's face looked a little flushed and after the doctor checked her for the last time, her worst fear came true. The fever was rising again. The doctor was just ready to tell Sofie that in good conscience he could not allow her to fly out, but when he looked at this beautiful woman who had suffered so much, he handed her the envelope with the letter that he had typed up for Sofie to give to the doctor when they got to their destination. He gave Emma one last shot and then he quickly turned around and walked away before Sofie could thank him again.

They went downstairs and got on the bus that took the people to the airport. The short ride seemed like hours, but finally they stood in front of a huge plane.

Everybody was given a gray blanket and again all the papers were checked. The guard looked at Emma's face. Then he said to Sofie in a harsh tone, "Is she all right? She looks feverish."

"Oh yes," Sofie answered. "It's the excitement. She has never seen an airplane and she has tired herself out just talking about it for days.

"All right then," the guard said. "You are good to go," and then he told them to board the plane.

It was a cargo plane. Two rows of benches on each side packed with people, no windows, but to Sofie it felt like a safe haven. She wrapped one blanket around Emma and the other around herself, and so they sat and waited until they heard the sound of the engines.

"Mama, why are you crying?"

"These are happy tears, Emma, happy tears. We are finally safe now."

Will they be?

Part II

Berlin

Sofia and Emma were on the plane that would take them to their new destination. The engine was roaring, getting ready for takeoff.

"We are finally safe," Sofie whispered to Emma, whose fever was rising again. "Just hold on, Emma," she told the child. "Just a few more hours and I will get you to a doctor." She touched the letter she held close to her chest that the doctor in Berlin gave her explaining that Emma was exposed to scarlet fever. "Everything will be all right, we are almost there." Again she looked at Emma's face. Emma was now sleeping. Then she looked up and realized that several people were staring at them.

One woman was saying to Sofie in a harsh voice, "Is she sick? Does she have the fever?" Then in an even louder voice she yelled, "I think we have a kid with the fever on the plane! We will all die if we don't get them off this plane!"

"Ladies, ladies," a steward from the front of the plane said, walking toward them. "What is going on here?"

"You let a girl with the fever on this plane! We are all going to die!" Several people were now yelling, "We need to get them off the plane!"

The steward was studying Sofie and Emma. Emma was asleep. "Let's move you two to the front of the plane. There is a little more room there, and the child can lie down," he told Sofie. Then he turned around to the rest of the passengers and said in a commanding tone, "Everybody sit down. I don't want to hear one word from any of you. We are in a airplane, miles away from land. Right now there is nothing any of you can do. Besides, the girl was checked by a doctor early this morning; she is just tired from the excitement.

"The next person that I see get out of their seat had better have a reason," he added, looking at the woman who was just getting ready to argue with him. "They will be reported upon landing to the authorities for putting a plane in jeopardy. Is this understood?" Nobody was saying a word. "Good," the steward said. Then he walked back to where Sofie and Emma were sitting.

"Thank you," Sofie said in a low voice.

"Make sure you get her to a doctor right away," the steward told her. Then neither of them said another word for the rest of the flight.

Finally they heard the landing gear. "Emma, wake up," Sofie told her daughter. "We are here. You will see your grandma in a little while. We are going to our new home."

"Everybody off the plane, form a line, you got to get instructions on what to do next," the voice from the speaker was saying. Sofie shuddered for a minute. There was another line, another paper check, how many more, but then she told herself, *this is different. We know where we are going.*

It was now their turn. "You need to come with me," a lady told Sofie as she pointed to another room.

Sofie was confused as she followed. "What is wrong?" she asked the lady.

"It's your mother-in-law. She was admitted to the hospital a week ago; that is why she could not be here. We have made arrangements for someone to take you to her home. Tomorrow you need to go to the courthouse to register. They will take care of your papers and tell you what you need to do next. I am so sorry," she added then. She nodded to another lady to take Sofie and Emma to the mother-in-law's house.

"Look, Emma, we will have our own bathroom." Sofie could not believe her eyes. It had been so long since she had been able just to lie and soak in a bathtub. The house was old, but very cozy and very well taken care of Sofie felt at home instantly. *Oh, we will be fine here,* she thought, looking at everything.

"Well, this is it for now." The voice of the woman who had brought them here ripped her out of her dreamy stage.

"Oh, I am sorry," Sofie told the lady. "Yes, we will be fine. Thank you for everything," and with that she walked the lady to the door.

"Emma, let me fix you something to eat. Then we'll take a bath and get a good night's sleep." Sofie looked at her daughter with worried eyes. "Tomorrow we will find a doctor and you will feel better soon." There was not much food in the house, but Sofie found two eggs and some bread, so they had their first meal in their new house.

Emma had taken her bath and was now fast asleep. Sofie sat on the sofa thinking about the last seven years. Then she heard a knock on her door. Startled, she got up. "Who is it?" she asked.

"It's Jacob, your brother," the voice said on the other side. Sofie opened the door. "Oh Jacob," she threw her arms around him, "I am so glad to see you, come in, come in."

Inside under the light, she almost went into shock when she looked at Jacob. This was not her handsome brother. The man in front of her had aged twenty years. He was so thin and tired-looking. All Sofie could recognize were his beautiful blue eyes, which looked so large, coming out of his thin face.

"Don't be shocked." He smiled at his sister. "I was a prisoner for a long time. I have only been released for about three months. You'll just have to fatten me up a little," he added with a smile as he wiped a tear from Sofie's face.

Then they started talking about the last seven years, until Jacob got up and said, "Enough for tonight. I will pick you and Emma up early tomorrow morning to visit Katrina." He hugged Sofie one more time. "Until tomorrow," he whispered and then he was gone.

As promised, Jacob picked Sofie and Emma up early the next morning to go to the hospital. Katrina's face lit up when she saw them, especially Emma, her son's only child. "She does not look sick," Sofie whispered to Jacob.

"We'll see," he told her, "the doctor wants to talk to us after the visit." An hour later they got the horrible news.

"Your mother-in-law has cancer. It has spread throughout her entire body. She has no more than two weeks to live."

How can this be? Sofie was in shock. "She looks so healthy—you must be mistaken."

"I wish that were the case," the doctor replied in a kind voice, "but often just before a patient dies they look and act as if nothing is wrong and that is the case here. I wish that I had better news for you," and with that, he left the room.

"He is wrong," Sofie told Jacob, but ten days later Katrina died.

Moving again

A few days after Katrina's funeral, her landlord knocked on Sofie's door. He introduced himself and then asked her what her plans were for the future, and if she intended to rent the house from him. Sofie had not even given it a thought, so much had happened in the last two weeks. She apologized and told him she would like to stay, but when he told her how much the rent was, she nearly fainted. "Wait a minute," she told him as he was ready to leave. "I will get a small amount from the government. It is about half of what you are asking for rent. Emma and I have to eat, so you can see it is impossible for me to pay this amount."

"Your loss then," he told her coldly. "You had best be out by the end of the month," and with that he left.

That afternoon Jacob came by and Sofie told him what had happened. "You need to go to your Contact Station and tell them your problem. They find places for the immigrants to live. You'll be fine." He tried to comfort her. "Things always work out, you'll see."

Things did work out. Sofie got an empty apartment that morning. The rent was cheap, and the lady told her, "When things get a little better, you can try to find something else. Would you like to see it? I can take you and show you the place."

"Oh, would you?" Sofie told her. "I only have nine days to be out of my mother-in-law's house."

"Well, let's go then," and so they went.

When they started walking toward a run-down building not far from the town's graveyard, Sofie said, "What is this?"

"Your new home if you decide to rent it. Four families live in the building. You don't have running water inside, but there is a pump outside where you can get your water. There is also an outhouse in the back. The city tries to clean it about every month.

"There is one bed in the apartment, also a hotplate and a couple of chairs. The rent is something that you can afford."

Sofie looked as if she were ready to cry, but she told the lady that she would take it. "I have no choice. At least Emma and I will have a roof over our heads."

"All right then, we will hold the rent out of your government check." She handed Sofie the key. "This way you can come and clean the place a little before you move in." Then she left.

Sofie studied the apartment a little while longer. There were two rooms, actually one room separated by some old heavy drapes for a little privacy. Oh, was it dirty! *I will have to clean it up before Emma sees it,* she thought. *Another change for you, Emma. Will it ever stop? But at least we are together. That is really what's most important.*

The Doctor

Emma was not feeling well, and it had been two weeks since Sofie made the appointment with the doctor for Emma. Finally they sat in his office waiting to see him.

He was a man in his fifties. Sofie felt uncomfortable with him right away. "I read your letter," he told her, "but I really don't see what I can do. You are not insured at this point and it is obvious that you don't have the money for any kind of treatment. I am wasting my time here," he added, and left the room.

Sofie sat on the chair in shock, not believing what had just happened. *This was no doctor, this was a monster,* she thought. And then she felt a hand on her arm; it was the nurse. "I heard every word," she told Sofie.

"He is a monster. He used to be a little kinder, but his son got killed in the war and he changed. But I will give you the name of another doctor. You will like him. I will also get in touch with him and tell him about Emma. So please make the appointment right away." Sofie thanked her and then she got Emma, who was still in another room, and they went home.

The Ring

Two days later they were sitting in the doctor's office again. Sofie was silently praying. *Please God, let this doctor help Emma, she is getting weaker every day.* When the door opened and they were sent into the examination room, Sofie watched nervously as the doctor examined Emma. "I have read the letter," he told her. "We do have a very sick little girl here. There is a new drug called penicillin, but it is not cheap, and at this point you have no insurance. The treatment will take weeks, maybe even longer."

"I have no money," Sofie interrupted, "but please, doctor, I have my mother's ring that she always wanted Emma to have. Please take the ring as payment for Emma's life." She reached around her neck, unfastened the rope, and handed the doctor the ring.

He looked at it. It was the most beautiful ring that he had ever seen. It was full of beautiful diamonds and worth a fortune. "Well, let's get the treatment started," he told Sofie as he gave Emma the first shot of penicillin.

That night after the doctor got home, he told his wife the story and handed her the ring. He thought that she would be excited, but the reaction he got was not at all what he expected. She looked at the ring for a long time, then handed it back to him with tears running down her face. "Right now I do not recognize the man I gave my heart to," she told him. "You became a doctor to make a difference and help people. This woman has lost everything, and is trying to save her child, and you took the last thing she had of her mother, who wanted the ring to go to her only grandchild. I would never be able to put it on my finger without feeling guilty. Has this war made you so heartless as to do this?"

He sat like a statue as he listened to his wife. *She is right,* he thought. *Has this war made me so cold?* A deep shame came over him. Would she ever forgive him? He knelt down in front of her with his head in her lap. "I will make it right," he told her. "Please forgive me. I will make it right."

She put her hand on his head and stroked his hair. Not a word was spoken. So they stayed for a very long time, each thanking God in their own way. Finally they got up and as they looked into each other's eyes they felt a closeness they had never felt before.

"I think that the medication is already starting to work," Sofie told the doctor on their next visit. "She is sleeping a little better and her appetite is coming back." Emma had gotten very thin.

"I am glad to hear this," he told them as he gave Emma her shot. Then he told Emma, "Go with the nurse, I need to talk to your mother for a few minutes." When the door closed behind them, the doctor reached into his pocket and handed Sofie the ring. "I need to give this back to you," he told her gently.

Sofie turned snow-white. "You are telling me you can't help Emma! You're telling me that you won't even try?"

"No, no, stop and listen to me. Emma is going to be fine. It will take a long time, but she will get well."

Then he had no choice but to tell her what had happened when he tried to give the ring to his wife. "I am still so ashamed. I hope you can also find it in your heart to forgive me."

Sofie was trying to hold back her tears. "There is nothing for me to forgive. Emma's life is the most important thing." She touched his hand, then left to get Emma.

What is wrong with him today? The two nurses looked at each other. They had not seen their boss act this happy for a very long time.

The Move

"We are going to live here."

"No way," Emma yelled when Sofie took her over to their new place. "Mama, it is a dump! We don't even have furniture, and no bathroom! What if I need to go in the middle of the night? I will die before I move here." Sofie tried to explain that this place was all they could afford, but Emma would not listen. "I hate you," she yelled at Sofie. Sofie saw the hatred in her daughter's eyes and it nearly broke her heart, but she said nothing. The evening went by and they still had not spoken. Finally Emma went behind the curtain and threw herself onto the bed.

What was that noise? Emma woke up. Where was her Mother? Then she heard it. She got out of bed and saw Sofie sitting in one of the old chairs, her head in her lap, crying uncontrollably. "Oh Mama," Emma ran to her. "Please don't cry. I am so sorry. I was so mean to you today. I don't hate you! I love you, please Mama, stop crying."

Sofie finally stopped. "Emma, it won't be forever," she told her child. "We will get out of here."

"I know, Mama, I know."

"Let's go and lie down and tomorrow we will face everything together." *She is growing up too fast,* Sofie thought as they lay on the small bed that came with the apartment. But as long as everything was all right between them, they would be strong enough to deal with whatever came next.

School

Emma loved school. Her grades were good and the other girls treated her fairly. She did not belong to the elite group; she lived on the wrong side of the tracks for that. So she pretty much stayed by herself.

One day in the lunchroom she saw Kulla, one of the richest and most popular girls in town, stare at her sandwich. Then she saw her get up and walk over to the table where she was sitting. "Is it okay if I sit and have lunch with you?" Emma was so surprised and so were the other girls. She nodded her head and pointed to the chair across the table. Kulla sat down and unwrapped her sandwich. Emma could not help but stare. The sandwich had meat piled an inch thick and cheese on top of it. Emma's, on the other hand, consisted of two pieces of bread.

Kulla had heard that Emma and her mom were really poor but she had never realized that they did not have enough to eat. She looked back at her sandwich and in a complaining voice, she said to Emma, "I don't know how many times I have told my mom not to pile so much meat on my sandwich. I can't eat this. Would you like to have some of it? Otherwise, I am going to trash it." Emma opened her two pieces of bread and watched Kulla put half of her meat on Emma's slices. They did not say much after that, but a friendship was born that would last a lifetime.

From that day on, Kulla shared everything with Emma. If she had two apples, she gave her one; if she had one, she would cut it in half. One day she came to the house with a table. It was my grandma's, she told Sofie. We don't have any use for it. If you don't want it, we will just have to throw it away. *Of course we wanted it, and so it became ours.*

Everything that Kulla could get her hands on, she would bring to the house, but she always acted as if we were doing her a big favor by taking it. And that was not all. Since Emma had befriended one of the most popular girls in town, she started getting birthday party invitations from the other girls and in a short time she was invited to everything with the so-called incrowd.

Money, Lots of Money

Emma was now sixteen and one day Sofie got a letter from the bank and the courthouse to set up a meeting with them. *I wonder what this is all about,* Sofie thought, but she had no choice, she had to go to the meeting.

Upon arriving at the bank, she was greeted by the head of the bank, who took her arm and gently walked her to his private office.

"Sit," he told her. "I have very good news for you. We have received records out of Poland about your husband's business and bank accounts. There is a buyer for the mill and the lumberyard with a very generous offer. Also the money from your accounts has been transferred to this bank and it is yours to do with as you please." He told her the amount and Sofie almost fainted.

She knew they had been rich back in Poland, but she really had no idea how rich. "Oh my God," was all she could say.

The banker just smiled. "Let me know what you decide about the business and if you want to sell it, this bank will be more than happy to handle all the transactions for you."

"I don't have to think about it," Sofie answered. "Please take care of everything for me. I know that we will never return to Poland, and even if we did I could not run the business. Yes, please take care of everything." With that, she got up to leave.

"Hold on a minute," the banker told Sofie. "Don't you want to leave the bank with some of your money in your pocket? You certainly have enough," he laughed.

"Yes, I would." Sofie did not fully understand her good fortune.

The banker left the office, but came back a few minutes later with a thick envelope of large bills and Sofie's bankbook. "Here you go," he said gently. "Buy anything you want for yourself and your daughter."

Sofie left the bank in a daze and went straight home. There she sat in the old chair holding her bankbook and staring in disbelief at the numbers.

We are really rich, she thought. *I can get enough food and clothes for Emma.* Still sitting, she heard Emma's voice outside the door. "Mama, I am home. What's to eat?..."

"We are going out to eat," Sofie told her daughter. "And then we are going shopping," she added. "You can have a new winter coat and shoes. Oh Emma, you can just have anything you want."

Emma looked at her mother. *She's gone crazy,* Emma thought, but Sofie twirled her around. "I will explain it all to you, but first we will go out to eat."

During dinner Sofie told Emma the whole story of what had happened that day. After that, the two women went shopping, but they hardly bought anything. It had been so many years that all they could do was look at the pretty things. They needed some time to realize that they could actually buy them. That evening, Sofie told Emma, "While you're in school tomorrow, I will start looking for a house for us on the right side of town, but let's go to bed now. I think that we have both had a very busy day."

The House

After Emma had left for school, Sofie got herself ready to start looking for a new place for them to live. She looked at several, but what she found was not really what she was looking for. Then she ended up in a brand-new neighborhood just starting to develop. She instantly fell in love with the street: Trees lined both sides. She kept walking and found herself standing in front of a house that was in its final building stage.

"Can I help you?" Sofie heard a man's voice.

"Whose house is this?" she asked.

"Nobody's yet," the man answered. "It will go on the market in a couple of weeks."

"May I go inside to look at it?"

The man looked at her, thinking. *She is poor, she cannot buy this house, but what harm can it do to let her see the inside.* "Sure, come with me," he told her. "I will walk you through it."

Sofie looked at everything. It had a private gate to keep strangers out. You also had to ring a bell and talk into a microphone before you could come in. So much privacy! Sofie was fascinated. It was exactly what she was looking for. "How much does this house cost?" she asked the man. He told her the price.

"I'll take it, but I want my daughter to see it when she comes home from school, she needs to love it as much as I do. So would it be all right if we came back this afternoon?"

"Sure." The man studied her again, not knowing what to think. This woman did not appear to have any money, but she did not look crazy. So he told her to bring her daughter in the afternoon. "I will be here to meet you." *I'll never see her again,* he thought as he watched

Sofie walk away. But he was wrong. Just as Sofie had told him, they came to see the house that afternoon.

Emma's eyes lit up when they walked through the house. "Oh Mama, it is beautiful. We will have our own bathroom." It was the bathroom that excited her the most.

"We'll take it," Sofie told the man, who still did not believe that this woman could buy this house.

"Well, let me get the papers ready," he told Sofie. "Then we'll have to meet with your bank to see if you can get the loan."

"That won't be a problem," Sofie reassured him. "We need to meet with my bank, but there will be no loan. I will pay cash for the house."

In total shock, the man nodded his head. "How about tomorrow," he told her. "I will meet you at your bank with all of the necessary papers."

"We are moving into a new house," Emma told her friend Kulla the next day. The two girls had truly became best friends.

"I am going to help you pack and move," Kulla replied. She was so happy for her friend.

The next two weeks went by much too slowly for Sofie and Emma, but Moving Day was finally here. "I cannot wait to take a bath," Emma told her mother. "I think I will stay in the tub forever." Sofie just smiled.

The new furniture also arrived on time. Sofie had purchased everything she thought they would need in the past two weeks—new beds, new sheets, new everything. Now if they would get a few groceries, they could stay at their new home for a couple of days and put everything where it needed to be.

Later that evening, "I am taking a bath, a very long bath," Sofie heard Emma say.

"Go ahead," Sofie replied, smiling to herself. How long had they dreamed about this? They were both so tired. It had been a long day, but a wonderful day. While Emma was soaking in the tub, Sofie walked through the rooms again and again. She was thanking God for this blessing.

Then it was Sofie's turn to soak in the tub, and finally both women went to sleep.

Emma's First Dance

Three times a year the town hosted a big dance. Old and young alike got to go to this. It was truly one of the great events. Big tents went up; the whole town was busy with excitement.

Emma was almost seventeen now and Sofie told her one evening that they were going to the dance. "Oh, Mama," Emma cried. "Is it true? I get to go? I really get to go?"

"Yes my darling, you will get to go," Sofie reassured her. "We will go shopping for a beautiful dress in the next few days, and shoes and whatever else we need."

"I need to go and tell Kulla," was the next thing Sofie heard Emma say, and then she watched through the window as her daughter ran down the street toward her best friend's house.

"I get to go to the dance," Emma told Kulla.

"Me too," her friend told her. "Oh, we are going to have so much fun!"

The next few days turned into major shopping days. Emma tried on so many dresses, but finally found the one she thought was the most beautiful. As Sofie watched her child's excitement she wondered where her little girl was, in front of her stood a young lady, a beautiful young lady. *Oh Michael,* she thought, *if only you could see your daughter. You would be so proud!* But then she stopped and told herself, *I cannot be sad. This is Emma's time and it needs to be a happy time.*

Finally it was the evening of the dance. The whole day Emma had fussed with her hair. Sofie was close to losing her patience a few times, but that too passed, and now the two women were on their way to the dance. Kulla and the other girls were already there waiting for Emma.

They had saved a seat for her at their table. "Look at all the good-looking men," Kulla whispered. "I am going to dance with every one of them." Emma saw one young man that she had seen in town many times and secretly admired. "I am only going to dance with him," she told Kulla.

Her best friend looked at her in surprise. "You are crazy, you need to dance with all of them."

Emma shook her head. "Those other boys don't interest me. I just want to dance with this one."

Finally the music started. The young men jumped out of their seats and ran toward the girls. Emma watched as her young man walked toward her. She thought her heart would jump out of her chest. She smiled. He was three steps away from her and then another young man took her hand and asked her to dance. As if she were in a trance, she followed him onto the dance floor, her eyes searching for the other one. "You are a wonderful dancer," her partner told her. "Did you have lessons?"

Emma looked at him. He was very handsome. "Yes I did," she told him.

Then he introduced himself. "I am Karl Mahan."

Mahan, Emma thought to herself. *I am dancing with the richest boy in town. His parents own practically the whole town, and he was every girl's dream. Actually every mother's dream for their daughters.*

As Emma kept dancing, she wondered, *Why am I not impressed, what is wrong with me? I should be so happy. He is very nice and good-looking. I should be happy,* but it changed nothing. Her eyes kept searching for the other man. Finally after a few more dances with Karl, she told him that she needed to sit down. She told him that she was thirsty. "I am so sorry," he apologized. "How selfish of me. I am having a hard time letting go, but let's sit down so I can get us some refreshments."

The music started again. Karl was still standing in line to get something to drink. Emma saw her dream man in front of her asking her to dance. She jumped up and followed him, her hand holding his. She looked into his eyes and listened to him as he told her that he had waited all night for this. When the music finally stopped, Emma felt as if she had just come out of a trance. All she could think was *Why did the music stop.*

Back at their table, Karl put his arm possessively around Emma's shoulders, and said, "There you are, darling. Here are our refreshments."

"Darling," Kulla whispered to her. "He is calling you darling in front of everybody. I don't believe this."

"You can have him," Emma hissed at her best friend. Her eyes were trying to find the other man.

Karl and Emma danced every dance together for the rest of the night. Emma had stopped having fun. She was ready to go home. Sofie had watched her daughter very closely all night. She was fully aware of what was going on in her little girl's heart.

Her own heart was heavy too. When Karl came back with the refreshments, he had told her that he was going to marry Emma. She was shocked, but then Sofie pulled herself together and told him, "Karl, how can you say this. You have just met her and besides, she is so young. She has never even dated, and she is going to college."

Karl just smiled. "I respect all that, Miss Sofie, and I will be patient, but Emma will be my wife."

"We should have never gone to that stupid dance, Mama. I was stuck with Karl all night," Emma complained the next day.

"Oh, it was just your first dance" Sofia told her. In six months, there will be another dance and everything will be different. Let's just forget the whole thing for now," and they both agreed on that.

But that proved to be easier said than done. The other girls started dating a little here and there with different boys, but nobody asked Emma out. "What is wrong with me?" she asked her best friend Kulla one day. "Nobody likes me. Do you have any idea why?"

"Yes, I know why and I will tell you why. When Karl was drafted into the army for basic training, he let everyone know that you and he were going to get married when he came back. You are spoken for."

Emma was stunned, then she got mad. "Oh, how dare he do such a thing! First of all, he had never even asked me. Second of all, I am not in love with him. Oh, I cannot believe this is happening to me. Don't you think you would have been the first to know if that was true? I thought you were my best friend!"

"Calm down," Kulla reassured her. "I am your best friend. Haven't I been trying to get you to go to some parties with us and you always say no."

"That is because everybody has a date and I don't. I don't like to be the fifth wheel. I told you that over and over. "Fine then," Emma said stubbornly. "I will go to the next party with you."

"Great, we are going to one tomorrow night."

Emma glared at her. "Tomorrow night it is." *What have I gotten myself into now? Emma asked herself. But I am not backing out, oh no, I am not backing out.*

The Party

Kulla, Emma, and several other boys and girls met to go together to the party. "Oh my, how many people are going to be here?"

"Lots," Kulla said. "It's a big house; there is room for lots of people." Emma was still in the foyer waiting for the maid to take her coat, when she felt a hand on her shoulder and a voice whispering.

"Where have you been for the last two months?" She looked up straight into the eyes of the man from the dance.

"Where did you come from?" That was all she could say.

"This is my mother's house, my two sisters are giving the party, and they insisted that I come. I almost did not, but now I am so glad I did. By the way, my name is Neal, and yours?"

"Emma," she replied.

"Emma." He looked at her. "It fits you."

They spent the whole evening together, talking, dancing, laughing. Emma hoped it would never end. "Can I see you tomorrow?" Neal asked when they were ready to leave.

"Yes," Emma said simply and smiled.

"Mama, wake up." Emma touched her mother's arm. Sofie was still awake; she really never slept solidly until she knew that Emma was home safe.

"Is something wrong?"

"Oh mama, nothing is wrong, I am in love. Remember the man from the dance? He was at the party tonight, and I am going to see him tomorrow."

She went on and on for the next hour, until Sofie knew every detail.

Neal and Emma saw each other every night and weekends for the next two months. Neal had fallen deeply in love with Emma. They played, they kissed, but they had never made love. One day Neal asked Emma to spend the night with him. "I want to hold you. I want to make love to you. I want to wake up with you. Please, Emma, spend the night with me."

Emma said yes. She felt ready and so they made wonderful plans for the coming weekend.

"Mama, can I spend the night over at Kulla's next weekend?" The girls had been spending many nights at each other's houses. "Kulla is having several girls over. We are having a slumber party." She felt guilty lying to her mother, but she could never tell her that she was going to spend the night with Neal.

"Of course you can," Sofie told her. She had never seen her child so happy.

The next day, Emma grabbed Kulla's arm. "I need your help! I am going to spend next Saturday with Neal, but I told Mama that I am spending it at your house for a slumber party. You need to cover for me, you are the only one that will know what I am doing." Kulla listened and then she became excited too. "I will cover for you. I wish I had some excitement in my life, you are having all the fun."

"Your time will come," Emma told her friend. "You just have not met the right man yet."

Saturday came and Emma packed her bag to go over to Kulla's. She was going to change clothes there before she went to Neal's. She was still feeling a little guilty about lying to her mother, but as soon as she saw Neal, she forgot about it.

Neal's place was warm and beautiful. He had cooked a wonderful dinner. They drank wine, danced, and laughed. They were the only two people in the world. Long after dinner, Neal poured them another glass of wine. Then he picked Emma up and carried her into his bed. Slowly, between long kisses, he removed her clothing piece by piece. "You are the most beautiful thing I have ever seen," he told her, "and you are mine."

"Yes, I am." She smiled as she watched him take off his clothes. Then he started to kiss her again, his fingers touching every inch of her body. When Emma thought she could stand no more he positioned himself and slowly entered her body. Emma let out a small cry. When she opened her eyes all she could see was Neal's face, which looked down at her in sheer horror.

"Neal, what's wrong," she whispered.

"You did not tell me you were a virgin. How could you not tell me," was all he said.

"I did not know it was a crime." Emma was crying by now, and beside, it only hurt a little bit.

"Oh my darling." Neal was back to his normal self. "You should have told me. I would have been more gentle. Let me just hold you for a little while." But soon passion took over for a second time and this time there was no holding back. So it went into the wee hours.

The next morning after Emma got back to Kulla's house, her friend wanted to know every detail. She too had never gone all the way with a man, but something in Emma was different. She told Kulla some of it, but the most important parts she kept to herself. It was only hers and Neal's.

Another two months went by. The lovers spent every minute they had in each other's arms. Nobody in town knew about them since Neal lived outside of town. Sofie watched Emma carefully, but she did not say anything. Her child would come to her when the time was right.

Another Dance

Six months had gone by and the town was getting ready for another dance. Karl was back home from his training. He stopped by several times to see Emma; he was also looking forward to the dance.

Three days before the dance, Neal was standing in the town's jewelry store looking at engagement rings. "That's the one," he told the storeowner. "Can you have this sized to a six by tomorrow?"

"I sure can," the man told him. "I have another engagement ring to size for Karl Mahan. He is also getting engaged, to that pretty little Emma Rech." Then he looked at Neal, whose face had turned white. "Are you all right?" he asked.

"Yes, thank you," Neal told him, "but I think I will wait on buying that ring."

"Suit yourself," the store owner told him as he watched Neal leave the store.

Back outside, Neal felt the bottom had just been pulled out from under him. His Emma getting engaged to another man. How could he have been so stupid.

That same night Emma waited for Neal, but he did not come to pick her up. When she did not hear from him by the next day, she got worried.

"I am going to see if Neal is all right," she told Sofie. "I am going to walk over to his house."

"It's a two-mile walk. Emma, be sure to be back home before it gets dark."

Neal watched Emma as she walked toward his house. He would never let her know how much she had hurt him.

When he opened the door Emma ran into his arms. "Oh Neal, I was so worried. Are you all right?"

He gently pushed her back. "I am fine," he told her, "but I am glad that you are here. I need to talk to you." Emma sat down and looked at him, not knowing what he had to tell her. "The truth is," he told Emma, "I have fallen in love with someone else. I am planning on marrying her."

What was he saying to her? The words did not make any sense. This could not be happening but when she looked at his face again, she slowly understood that this was not a bad dream. He had fallen in love with someone else.

She slowly got up from the chair and walked to the door. Neal watched her. His heart was breaking. Should he run after her? But his pride took over. No, she would not make a fool of him a second time. Later Emma did not remember how she had gotten home. Sofie started to ask but Emma stopped her. "Not now, Mama. I am going to bed."

"The dance is tomorrow night. What do you mean you're not going?" Kulla was now getting really upset. "Karl reserved the best table for us. You have to go. The town has also invited some American soldiers to the dance. Maybe I will meet Mr. Right."

Emma put her hand over Kulla's mouth. "All right, I am going. Don't talk about it anymore."

"You are so moody, Kulla told her, but at least you're going. It will be fun, you'll see."

Karl was already at their table when the girls arrived. He put his arm around Emma and told her to sit next to him.

Emma was ready to tell him that he had no right to give her orders, but held her tongue. Her friends flirted and started dancing with some of the American soldiers. Everybody looked as if they were having a really good time. There was one soldier who kept looking at Emma and when the music started again, he got up from his chair and walked toward Emma's table.

Karl watched him and then told Emma that he had better not ask her to dance with him. Anger welled up in her and when the soldier asked her, she jumped out of her chair and followed him. They danced that dance and the next, and next. Emma almost felt joy when she saw Karl's angry face. When she returned to their table, Karl stood up, clapped his hands and asked everyone to be quiet. "I have an announcement to make." The room got so quiet you could have heard a needle drop. Then Karl turned to Emma with the engagement ring and announced their engagement.

Emma was so shocked she felt the blood draining from her face. She thought about how Neal had hurt her. And now this. Then pure anger took over. She turned to Karl and with a firm voice told him that she did not love him and that she would never marry him. She then grabbed her purse and her coat and left the tent. Nobody tried to stop her or Kulla, who was running behind her.

"Oh Emma," Kulla told her. "You just made a big mistake, a very big mistake. Karl will make sure that nobody in this town will ever ask you out again."

"I don't care." Emma was so mad she was crying now. "I don't care. I never wanted to get married anyway." But it turned out to be even worse than Emma could have imagined.

When she went into town the next day, people looked away as if she had the plague. She had done the unthinkable. She had publicly insulted the son of the richest man in town. Kulla had been right. Nobody would ever ask her out again.

Two days later the doorbell rang at Sofie's house. When Emma looked out she saw the American soldier from the dance standing outside her door. "You were very hard to find," he told her, with a mischievous twinkle in his eyes. "Especially since you only gave me your first name. But would you like to go somewhere and have some ice cream?"

"Yes I would," Emma replied. Then to herself she added, *I'll show this town.*

They went and Emma found herself having more fun than she had thought possible. That first date turned into many more and when Robert asked her to marry him two months later, she said yes.

Sofie's heart was heavy when she heard the news. Her little girl was going so far away, but she also knew that Emma would not change her mind. *I'll start making plans for the wedding.* Then she told Emma, "Under one condition. I want you to go to America and meet Robert's family. I need to know that you are welcome there and when you come back, we will have a big, beautiful wedding."

Robert agreed to this. He told Sofie that he had a thirty-day leave coming. It would be long enough for Emma to meet all of his family. And so it was.

Three weeks later, Sofie and Kulla watched as the plane took off to take Emma on her first flight to America.